# That's Mine, That's Yours

## Angie Sage and Chris Sage

VIKING

**VIKING**
Published by the Penguin Group
27 Wrights Lane, London W8 5TZ, England
Viking Penguin, a division of Penguin Books USA Inc. 375 Hudson Street, New York, New York 10014, USA
Penguin Books Australia Ltd, Ringwood, Victoria, Australia
Penguin Books Canada Ltd, 2801 John Street, Markham, Ontario, Canada L3R 1B4
Penguin Books (NZ) Ltd, 182-190 Wairau Road, Auckland 10, New Zealand

Penguin Books Ltd, Registered Office: Harmondsworth, Middlesex, England

First published 1991
10 9 8 7 6 5 4 3 2 1

Copyright © Angie Sage and Chris Sage, 1991

The moral right of the author and illustrator has been asserted

Filmset in Baskerville
Printed in Hong Kong
A CIP catalogue record for this book is available from the British Library
ISBN 0-670-83746-6

me          you

Look, I've found my sweater

And you've found your shirt

That's mine,

sweater

pants

tights

underpants

that's yours.

shirt

diaper

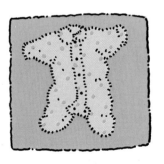
suit

socks

Look what's in our toy-box…
this is your car,
this is your ball,
these are your blocks
and this is your blanket.

car

ball

blocks

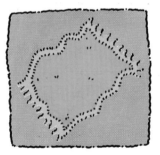

blanket

But that's my book
you're holding.

book

This is your train,
this is your fish,
this is your teddy
and this is your dog.

train

fish

teddy

dog

But that's my duck
you're playing with.

duck

Can I have my duck now…please?

YOU GIVE IT BACK!

Look, here's my rabbit!

Do you want my rabbit?

It was mine when
I was small,
but you can have
it now.

rabbit

It's lunchtime!
You can sit in your chair.
Here's your spoon and your bib,
your mug and your bowl.
Would you like some cereal and milk,
or a cookie?

chair          spoon          bib          mug

bowl          cereal          milk          cookie

I can sit at the table.
I have a plate, a cup and a fork.
That's my apple you're eating.
It's not yours, it's mine!
I'm having a hot dog, toast,
orange juice and that apple
for my lunch.

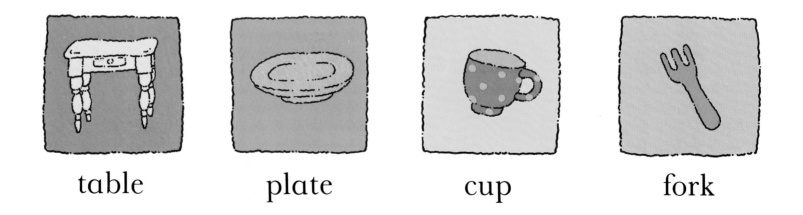

table      plate      cup      fork

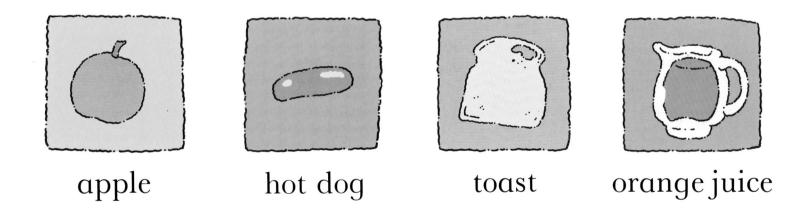

apple        hot dog        toast        orange juice

Let's go outside!
We both need our
hats, scarves,
boots and mittens.

hat

scarf

boots

mittens

Look, here's your ball and your swing,
that's my tree-house.
The tree-house is too high for you,
so let's play in the leaves!

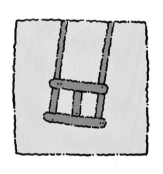

ball      swing      tree-house      leaves

I'm tired…let's get ready for bed.
We can go up to your bedroom.
Here's your crib and your quilt,
there are your slippers and your teddy.

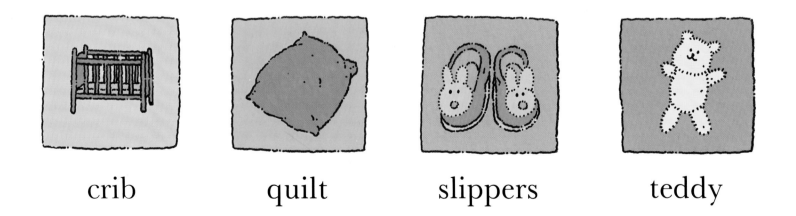

crib     quilt     slippers     teddy

Night-night…sleep tight.